Collins
MUSIC

PRIMARY MUSIC LEADER'S
HANDBOOK

T0340430

INSPIRING IDEAS
DR ELIZABETH STAFFORD

William Collins' dream of knowledge for all began with the publication of his first book in 1819.

A self-educated mill worker, he not only enriched millions of lives, but also founded a flourishing publishing house. Today, staying true to this spirit, Collins books are packed with inspiration, innovation and practical expertise. They place you at the centre of a world of possibility and give you exactly what you need to explore it.

Collins. Freedom to teach.

An imprint of HarperCollins*Publishers*
The News Building
1 London Bridge Street
London
SE1 9GF

HarperCollins*Publishers* Macken House
39/40 Mayor Street Upper
Dublin 1
DO1 C9W8
Ireland

collins.co.uk

Text © HarperCollins*Publishers* 2021

© HarperCollins*Publishers* 2021

10 9 8 7 6 5 4 3

ISBN 978-0-00-851878-3

British Library Cataloguing in Publication Data

A catalogue record for this publication is available from the British Library.

Author: Dr Elizabeth Stafford
Commissioning editor: Naomi Cook
Development editor: Em Wilson
Proofreader: Ann Barkway
Cover image: Ansis Klucis/Shutterstock
Cover design: Fresh Lemon Australia
Internal design: Fresh Lemon Australia
Production controller: Lyndsey Rogers
Printed and bound by Ashford Colour Press Ltd

The external web links have been included for convenience of the users and were checked at the time of publication, but the Publisher is not responsible for the content of external sites and cannot guarantee that links continue to work or that the quality of the content has been maintained. The links are not intended to form part of the product and have been included purely for educational purposes. It is the user's responsibility to ensure the external web links meet their requirements.

MIX
Paper | Supporting responsible forestry
FSC
www.fsc.org
FSC™ C007454

This book contains FSC™ certified paper and other controlled sources to ensure responsible forest management.

For more information visit: www.harpercollins.co.uk/green

Acknowledgements

Thank you to Jonathan, who makes everything I do possible, and Isla who makes everything I do worthwhile.

My thanks also to the team at Music Education Solutions®, the editing team at Collins Music, and anyone else who has ever shown an interest in the things I have to say about music education!

For their inspiration, support and friendship throughout my career, grateful thanks to Professor Martin Fautley, Dr Ally Daubney, and Gary Spruce.

Contents

Introduction

Congratulations! You have been given the role of primary music leader. Maybe you asked for it, maybe you did not, maybe you are 'musical', maybe you are not, but the job is yours! Perhaps you have been in the role for a while and are looking for some inspiration, or this could be a brand new role and you are wondering how to get started. Whether you are relishing or dreading the responsibility, this handbook and its accompanying online resources have been written to support you in this challenging but rewarding role.

This handbook will support you to develop all aspects of music in your school, whatever your starting point. It will help you to analyse and audit your current music provision in order to identify areas for improvement, and create an action plan to address these. You can read it from cover to cover or dip in and out, returning to whichever sections you need to re-read throughout your time in the role.

Chapter 1

Preparing for the role

In this chapter you will find out what the role of a music subject leader entails, and the key knowledge you will need to perform the role successfully.

- **What is the role of primary music leader?**

- **Curriculum music – what do you need to know?**
  - Skill areas
  - Elements of music
  - Notation
  - Styles, genres, traditions and periods

- **Extra-curricular music role**
  - Organising instrumental lessons
  - Providing a programme of extra-curricular activities
  - Organising shows and performances
  - Inviting musicians into school

- **Where to find help**

- **Balancing the role with your other commitments**

What is the role of primary music leader?

A primary music leader is responsible for ensuring that the music curriculum is planned, delivered, and assessed effectively. This will involve:

- **creating a vision for music – deciding what music is 'for' in your school**
- **designing (or sourcing) and resourcing the music curriculum**
- **supporting your colleagues to deliver the curriculum**

In England, the primary music leader may be expected to take part in a music 'deep dive' process as part of an Ofsted inspection, where they will need to demonstrate the effectiveness of the curriculum to the inspector.

Unlike in other subjects, where the subject leader role is concerned only with curriculum, the role of music subject leader is also likely to involve:

- **overseeing a programme of extra-curricular activities**

You may be starting from the position of a 'specialist' with a degree or other qualifications in music, an 'enthusiast' with a love of all things musical, or a complete novice with perhaps a borderline fear of music! Whatever your level of musical experience, the role has the same core requirements, and this book aims to help you 'fill the gaps' where necessary.

Curriculum music – what do you need to know?

The expectation is that all primary teachers have excellent pedagogical understanding of all the subjects that they teach. But in reality we know that this is not always the case, and particularly so in the case of music! The 'foundation subjects' are traditionally not given a great deal of attention in ITE (Initial Teacher Education) where the focus tends to be firmly on the 'core' subjects of English and maths. This means that many primary teachers rely on their own education for their understanding of the foundation subjects. Given that currently only around 5,000 students take A-level music each year, and around 35,000 take GCSE (Cultural Learning Alliance), this means that in all likelihood the majority of your school's teachers will have 'dropped' music at the end of KS3.

What all this means is that to be an effective music subject leader, you need to develop a strong musical understanding so that you can support your colleagues who may be less confident or expert in music. This doesn't mean that you have to be a music 'specialist' with a degree or Grade 8 qualification. All the knowledge and skills you need can be learnt on the job!

Skill areas

Most schools are required to follow some form of prescribed national curriculum. Although the specifics of each devolved nation's national curriculum differ, they all cover the same broad skill areas:

- **listening to music**
- **performing (singing and with instruments)**
- **improvising and composing music**

And, they aim to build:

- **theoretical understanding** – gaining some theoretical knowledge around the way music functions, its place in history, and its communication systems (for example, musical notations, including staff notation)

Top tip

Although you might not think it, being a 'non-specialist' may give you an advantage over a music specialist in that you will know first-hand how a less confident musician can develop their knowledge to become more confident in teaching music, which will help you design more effective support systems for your colleagues.

Elements of music

Music is made up of key elements or building blocks, which are combined together to create an artistic effect. In England these are referred to as the 'inter-related dimensions of music' to encourage teachers and children to consider how they work together rather than in isolation.

The elements of music

Element	Definition
Pitch	The sound frequency of a note (high/low)
Duration	The length of a note (long/short)
Dynamics	The volume of the music (loud/quiet)
Tempo	The speed of the music (fast/slow)
Timbre	The quality or 'colour' of sound (what makes different instruments and voices sound unique), e.g. 'bright', 'dark', 'warm'
Texture	The number of layers within the music (thick/thin)
Structure	How the music is organised (sections)

This table is available online alongside some common associated vocabulary and their definitions (see online resources).

Notation

While your first thought when you read the word 'notation' may be staff notation – the lines and dots that make up the communication system developed for Western classical music – 'notation' can actually encompass *any* method of writing music down.

For example, in a primary school you are likely to use:

• **'letter notation' – where instead of using staff notation you write down the letter names of the notes to be played**

• **'graphic notation' – where you draw images to represent the different sounds in the music**

There are no hard and fast rules when using these types of notation, whereas 'official' systems like staff notation do require you to work within prescribed parameters. Below we have provided some brief guidance for how staff notation works.

Staff notation

Unless you are very lucky, you will probably find that most of your colleagues do not read staff notation. This is not as much of a problem as people think it is; the ability to 'read' music has no real bearing on your ability to 'teach' music. Where it becomes problematic is when you are working with a national curriculum or other system which has expectations related to staff notation – such as the national curriculum in England which states that KS2 children should "use and understand staff and other notations". As primary music leader, it may therefore be useful for you to gain a basic understanding of the staff notation signs and symbols that you might use when teaching notation at primary level.

Treble stave

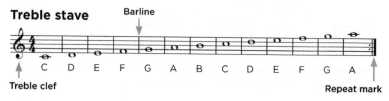

Bass stave

Time signature: the top number shows the number of beats in the bar; the bottom number shows the type of beat, for example:

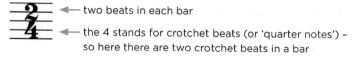

← two beats in each bar

← the 4 stands for crotchet beats (or 'quarter notes') – so here there are two crotchet beats in a bar

Barline: divides the music into bars of a certain number of beats, corresponding to the time signature.

Repeat mark: tells you to go back and repeat that section of the music.

Note symbols in 4/4

Semibreve (lasts four beats)

Minim (lasts two beats)

Crotchet (one beat)

Quaver (half a beat)

Sometimes groups of quavers and semiquavers are 'beamed' together.

Semiquaver (quarter of a beat)

Dots: a dot after a note increases the length of the note by half, for example:

this note is three beats: two-beat note (minim) + one beat

Styles, genres, traditions and periods

One of the most important aspects of a subject leader's role is to ensure that the curriculum is broad and inclusive, and particularly in the case of music that it encompasses a wide variety of music from all around the world. As primary music leader you will need to understand how music is classified, in order to ensure that your curriculum has suitable breadth.

Key knowledge: Styles, genres, traditions and periods

Style	Style is a term for music that has recognisable features and characteristics. For example: 'jazz music' would include a range of individual styles such as Dixieland and Swing.
Genre	An umbrella term for music from a wide range of styles that are linked by purpose. For example: 'film music' would be a genre that would encompass the individual styles of 'hollywood' film music, Bollywood music, etc.
Tradition	A tradition is a type of music that contributes to national identity. For example: in England we might refer to 'sea shanties' as a musical tradition; in Trinidad 'calypso' is a musical tradition.
Period	A period is a point in time during which composers adopted similar rules, structures and effects in their music. It is most often associated with Western classical music in which the main periods are: • Medieval (c. 1150–1400) • Renaissance (c. 1400–1600) • Baroque (c. 1600–1750) • Classical (c. 1750–1830) • Romantic (c. 1830–1920) • Modern (c. 1920 to the present day)

Extra-curricular music role

For a subject like music, the subject leader role is likely to involve responsibility for an extra-curricular programme as well as the curriculum. This may include:

- organising instrumental lessons
- providing a programme of extra-curricular activities, such as ensembles and choirs
- organsing shows and performances
- inviting musicians into schools

Organising instrumental lessons

You might think organising instrumental lessons is a simple task – you ring up your local music service and ask for a teacher, then sit back and relax! However, there are a great number of tasks that need to be undertaken if your instrumental lesson programme is going to be successful.

Firstly you will need to decide whether you want to buy in an external provider (such as an instrumental music service) or whether you want to contract an individual teacher either on a self-employed or employed basis. This decision will need to be taken in conjunction with your school business manager, as there are legal and financial ramifications for each option that need to be thought through. There have recently been a number of high-profile cases of instrumental teachers winning legal challenges regarding their employment status, so you need to be sure from the start that you are setting your teachers up correctly.

If you decide on an external provider, by and large you can avoid the legal issues outlined above, and you may also find that there are additional benefits, such as:

- direct billing of parents
- timetable creation
- instrument hire and external practice diaries being rolled into the provision
- easier access to external progression routes such as ensembles, and performance opportunities in your wider community
- training – you may find that the teacher is highly trained and receiving regular CPD through their employer, so is up to date with all the latest music and general educational trends and requirements

However, you will retain very little 'control' over the teacher, may possibly be assigned a new teacher every year, and may not be able to build up the relationship between the instrumental teacher and the school as you would like due to the fact that they may well be dashing off to another school immediately after visiting you. You might also find that if pupil numbers drop, an external service may not consider your provision viable, and will require a minimum number of hours per week in order to confirm a booking. In this situation you may decide that contracting an individual teacher will suit your needs better, but do remember that if you do this then aside from the legal ramifications you will also need to consider providing them with resources and training if you want them to stay up to date and effective.

Wherever your instrumental teacher comes from, as primary music leader it will most likely fall to you to ensure that they have everything that they need to teach successfully in your school. This means:

- **Providing a suitable room for the teacher to teach in – not a thoroughfare, a shared space or a cupboard!**
- **Promoting the lessons to children (and parents), and ensuring they know when lessons take place**
- **Letting the instrumental teacher know of any changes to pupils or lesson times well in advance so that they can prepare**
- **Providing performance opportunities for their pupils, and possibly helping with the administration associated with entering for graded exams**
- **Being a point of contact for the instrumental teacher – someone with whom they can discuss any issues or concerns regarding their teaching at the school**

Top tip

Although you are very likely to be teaching yourself when the instrumental teacher is in school, finding some time to check in with them regularly – even if it is only five minutes at the end of the day – can be really valuable in building up relationships and ensuring that the instrumental provision reflects your overall vision for music across the school.

Providing a programme of extra-curricular activities

Although the role of a subject leader is to lead on curriculum, with music being a performing arts subject, there is likely to be an expectation that you organise an extra-curricular programme of clubs and ensembles, alongside the instrumental lessons mentioned above, and the shows and performances we will talk about in a moment. All of this can add up to a considerable amount of extra work so you need to be careful how much you take on.

Top tip

Just because you have programmed an extra-curricular ensemble it doesn't mean you have to run it yourself! There may be other members of staff who would love to be in charge of the choir, or one of your instrumental teachers could be paid to deliver a lunchtime orchestra or after school band.

In Chapter 7 we look in detail at how you can construct an extra-curricular programme that supports your overall vision for music in your school (see page 67).

Organising shows and performances

As primary music leader, it is extremely unlikely that you will get away without being roped into every single performance that takes place! A performance is not a performance without music, so whether or not the central purpose of the event is to be a 'music event' you will doubtless find yourself helping out in some way. Remember though that the history subject leader is not being asked to train the choir for the nativity, provide some drummers for a school open day and organise a concert to showcase all the instrumental learners in the school! You are only one person, and the most important part of your role is the curriculum aspect, so if your school has a lot of performance events that are causing you stress, you should talk to your SLT about what is reasonable to expect you to take on. (More advice on this in Chapter 7, page 70.)

Inviting musicians into school

Listening to music is an important part of any music curriculum, and it is likely that you will want to mix things up a little where possible by inviting musicians into school to perform to your pupils rather than just listening to recorded music all of the time. Most schools get hundreds of unsolicited marketing contacts every year from organisations keen to sell them 'workshops' or other activities, and it can be a tricky task to sort the wheat from the chaff.

When booking a musician or ensemble for your school you should consider:

• How 'participatory' is the offer? – Is it just a concert or are there opportunities for your pupils to interact with the music and musicians?

• Is it linked to your national curriculum, and if so how specific are the links? – Any concert could claim a link to the skill area of 'listening' but what is this opportunity providing in detail beyond this?

• How experienced are the musicians and do other schools or music organisations endorse them?

• Are the musicians DBS checked and have they had appropriate safeguarding and equality, diversity and inclusion training for the activity that they are intending to provide?

• How 'bespoke' is their offer? – Can you request that it covers certain aspects which link to your curriculum, is targeted at a certain group of children, or is a specific length or format?

• Is their offer 'authentic'? – Will it give a real flavour of that particular musical style or tradition, or has it been diluted to suit the musician or ensemble in question?

• Do the musicians reflect your school community? – It is important for young people to 'see themselves' represented in the adults who teach them, so over time you will want to ensure that a range of visitors from different backgrounds have been visible in your school.

Top tip

Having real live musicians come into school can be extremely exciting and memorable for your pupils, but you will also want these experiences to be educational – especially if you are spending a significant amount of money!

Where to find help

The job of primary music leader can be a lonely one, and many research studies have acknowledged that both primary and secondary music leaders often feel professionally isolated. You may be the only 'musician' in your school with no one else to bounce ideas off, or of course you may not be a 'musician' at all, and feel that you have nowhere to turn for support. If either of these is the case then you will want to look beyond your school to the wider music education community for support and advice.

Literature and podcasts

This handbook is a starting point to supporting you in your role, but there is a wealth of other texts out there waiting to be discovered.

- **Books:** For teaching ideas try the rest of the *Inspiring Ideas* series from Collins Music (**collins.co.uk/pages/inspiring-ideas**), or to delve deeper into theory and pedagogy then anything written by Keith Swanwick, Janet Mills or John Paynter is a must.

- **Research:** To keep on top of contemporary research then keep an eye out for anything published by Professor Martin Fautley (@DrFautley) and/or Dr Ally Daubney (@AllyDaubney) who are the go-to researchers (both separately and collaboratively) for most of the UK's music education organisations and subject associations.

- **Articles:** For a range of articles on a variety of topics relating to primary music, check out *Primary Music Magazine* which is published once a term and is free to access (**issuu.com/primarymusicmagazine**).

- **Podcasts:** If you are more of a listener than a reader then *The Music Education Podcast* hosted and produced by Chris Wood is a really informative and entertaining series covering a range of issues including policy and advocacy (**soundstorm-music.org.uk/news/podcast**).

Support networks

To combat that feeling of professional isolation, find a support network to join. In England, your local music education hub or your Multi-Academy Trust (MAT) probably has a music network group that you can join with regular meetings you can attend. If one does not exist in your area then why not get together with a cluster of schools to form your own? As an alternative or an addition, there is a plethora of excellent primary music groups on Facebook that you can join to receive, and share, advice and support.

Professional associations

Joining a professional music association might be worthwhile for you, especially if you are keen to use this to show that your school is serious about music. These include:

- Music Mark – **musicmark.org.uk**
- Incorporated Society of Musicians (ISM) – **ism.org**
- Scottish Association for Music Education (SAME) – **same.org.uk**
- Society for Music Education in Ireland (SMEI) – **smei.ie**
- International Society for Music Education (ISME) – **isme.org**

Conferences

A conference can be a great way to top up your training, but make sure you look for one that offers you plenty of opportunity for discussion and networking with other delegates, as this is often the most valuable part of the day!

The *Curriculum Music Conference* run by Music Education Solutions® is focused solely on music in the curriculum and brings together subject leaders from right across the UK (**musiceducationsolutions.co.uk/events**).

The UK's biggest national conference is the *Music and Drama Education Expo* organised by the Mark Allen Group. This event brings virtually the entire music education sector into one London venue across two days. While the session programme has to cater for all delegates, meaning limited primary-only options, the event is worth attending for the trade fair alone, where you can browse thousands of resources (**musicanddramaeducationexpo.co.uk**).

CPD courses

There are an overwhelming number of organisations offering live and online CPD courses for music education, and it would be easy to become bogged down in the decision-making process! Fortunately the DfE in England commissioned the Teacher Development Trust (TDT) to prepare a set of 'Standards for teachers' professional development', which provide a useful framework to help you decide which CPD options to go for.

The standards quite rightly state that you should first and foremost consider the potential impact on pupil outcomes. This does not mean that the course always needs to be about 'teaching pupils something'. You might get better pupil outcomes in the long run by sending their teacher for a series of singing lessons, or offering the KS2 teaching team some music theory lessons. For maximum effect, professional development options should be selected based on issues and ideas arising from teachers' own reflective practice. Later in this book we will cover some ideas for helping teachers reflect on their own musical knowledge and understanding (see page 57).

Another key consideration listed in the standards is to ensure that any CPD that you select is underpinned by evidence and expertise. For music this means ensuring that any course or programme that you select is based on research evidence, rather than just the experience of the course leader, or the 'method' of any resource that the course may be trying to 'sell' you. Look for options that respect your professionalism as a teacher, and give you the 'why' behind the 'what' of the content. Otherwise you run the risk that when the activity you learnt on the course does not work with your class, you don't have any strategies for an alternative approach.

Bearing the above considerations in mind, you could approach the following organisations to find out about the CPD that they offer or the providers that they would recommend:

- **your local music education hub**
- **your local university or teacher training provider**
- **your local or national music subject association**
- **the MAT that your school belongs to** (where relevant)
- **your local authority school improvement team**

Reading recommendation

You can find the *Standards for teachers' professional development* at **gov.uk/government/publications/standard-for-teachers-professional-development**.

Balancing the role with your other commitments

Unless you are very lucky, the role of primary music leader is unlikely to come with additional remuneration such as a Teaching and Learning Responsibility post (TLR), so a lot of the effort you put in will be based on your own goodwill. As teachers we all want to do our best at all times, but we also need to prioritise our own class (if we have one), and most importantly look after ourselves.

It is important to remember that unlike many other subjects, the subject leader role in music is likely to include a large amount of extra-curricular responsibility as well as the main part of the role dealing with the curriculum. What you want to avoid is giving up every single lunchtime to supervise a music club or ensemble and then also teaching a full timetable. I can guarantee that the geography subject leader has no such problems!

When we also factor in the fact that music is one of the subjects that teachers often feel least confident about, and that due to its practical nature, supporting staff is going to require a lot more team teaching and observation than other subjects, this all adds up to an awful lot of extra work over and above what is expected of other subject leaders.

To be an effective subject leader for music, what you will need is time. Your Senior Leadership Team (SLT) should work with you to find a balance between your day-to-day responsibilities and your subject leader role so that you are provided with the time that you need to fulfil the role effectively. If your school is just starting out on its music improvement journey, you might need a considerable amount of time to get everyone up to speed, which may then reduce over subsequent years once everyone is settled into the curriculum and their teaching.

Top tip

Don't be afraid to ask your SLT for the time that you need – after all, there's no point having a subject leader at all if they are not given the time to actually do the job!

Chapter 2

Creating a vision for music in your school

In this chapter you will consider the role of music in your school, and start to think about creating your own music 'vision'.

- **Defining your vision**

- **Aligning with the School Improvement Plan**

- **Creating your vision statement**
  - The three I's sandwich

- **Communicating your vision**
  - Communicating your vision to staff
  - Communicating your vision to children
  - Communicating your vision to parents/carers

Defining your vision

"Ultimately, it is for us to imbue our students with an understanding of our subjects that goes beyond their school experience in a way that pays service to both the beauty and the sophistry of the subject. 🔊"
Howard and Hill

The starting point for any primary music leader is the question: 'why are we doing music?' Before you can make decisions about curriculum content, assessment strategies, or delivery models, you must first consider what you want your children to get out of studying music. Each school will have their own take on the purpose of music, but some ideas might include:

- Giving children a lifelong love of music
- Developing children's musical skills so they can participate in musical activities now and in the future
- Preparing children for further musical study at secondary school
- Developing children's self-confidence, teamwork and leadership skills
- Helping children encounter and learn to respect music from a wide range of cultures
- Meeting the requirements of the national guidelines for music in your country
- Developing children's creative thinking and self-expression
- Giving children the chance to participate in musical activities that would otherwise be unavailable to them

Once you have decided what *you* think the purpose of music is, it is important to then consult with colleagues and children to find out what they think too. That way you can come up with a vision for music that encompasses the needs of your whole school community.

As you know from your own experience, teachers are extremely busy people, and while they might be genuinely interested in your vision for music, they may not have the time or headspace to engage with this properly. Your best bet is probably to take five minutes in a staff meeting to present your vision as bullet points and ask if anyone disagrees or has comments to add. You can then make it clear that there is the option to give further comments for a limited time period (perhaps one week) if anything occurs to them after the meeting, but after this the vision will be established and accepted as school policy.

Top tip

Engaging children meaningfully in a consultation process can be tricky. In one of my schools we asked children what new playground equipment they would like, and the top vote went to a swimming pool full of jelly! Like any activity you need to make this consultation process accessible but also meaningful. Try:

- A 'mood board' with questions that the children stick their answers to on sticky notes
- Raising this as an item in a pupil council meeting (where your more 'sensible' children are likely to be in the right frame of mind to contribute meaningfully!)
- Having a 'focus group' where you make your vision 'real' for the pupils by giving them a taster of what it actually means, and asking them if they think anything is missing

Aligning with the School Improvement Plan

Once you have established your vision for music in your school, the next step is to try and tie this in with your overall School Improvement Plan (SIP). The cynical reason for this is that subjects which are directly connected to the SIP are taken more seriously, and are less likely to be forgotten about when it comes to budget, timetabling, and teaching!

But cynicism aside, music is almost always going to be the perfect fit for your school improvement aims. Why? Because there are so many studies showing that music has many benefits to learning, wellbeing, and skill development beyond the subject itself. You will easily find a link between music and the aims of your SIP, whether it concerns literacy or numeracy, personal development, communication and language development, or any other area of concern.

> **"There is more to music education than learning and memorising songs, or the technical aspects of playing an instrument. While these are important skills to develop, there is much more that must be imparted to our music students.** Fisher

Teachers working in England, and subject to Ofsted inspections, may well find that the phrases 'cultural capital' and 'transferrable skills' have worked their way into the SIP. Music provides the perfect vehicle for increasing both cultural capital and transferrable skills, though not necessarily at the same time!

- **Cultural capital** – Listening to a wide range of music from different cultures and traditions will not only broaden children's horizons but will increase their cultural capital – provided that the music listened to is 'the best' of its particular style or tradition.

- **Transferrable skills** – Any practical music-making activity is going to develop transferrable skills such as teamwork, leadership, presentation, creative thinking and so forth.

Reading recommendation

The Power of Music by Professor Susan Hallam is one of the key research texts that all primary music leaders should read to understand the many possible varied benefits of music on children's learning, wellbeing, and development.

Creating your vision statement

Although many primary schools have music policies or vision statements, there is no requirement from Ofsted or the Department for Education (DfE) for your music overview to be in a particular format. (The only statutory requirement in England is to ensure that a year-by-year breakdown of your curriculum is available on your school website, and this can be presented in any format.) This means that you theoretically have ultimate flexibility for how you create your music vision statement/overview, although in practice your school will probably have a specific template that they want you to use.

However you decide to structure your vision statement, you may find it useful to think about Ofsted's three I's: 'Intent', 'Implementation' and 'Impact'. While these terms are generally used in relation to the curriculum, they can be applied to the bigger picture of music as a whole in your school, to include extra-curricular activities.

The three I's sandwich

The middle I, 'Implementation,' is very much about how you deliver your vision, and you might not have thought about this yet (there is lots of advice for developing your implementation strategy in the remaining chapters of this book). However, the other two – 'Intent' and 'Impact' – are worth thinking about now, and will in fact help you to decide how you then go about implementing music in your school.

Intent, Implementation and Impact

Intent
The 'big picture' of music in your school – what it is for and how it will benefit your children, including how it contributes to the School Improvement Plan.

Implementation
How you will achieve what you intend – what activities and resources will be available.

Impact
What children will be able to do when they leave your school – often best expressed as bullet points.

Communicating your vision

If you involved your colleagues and children in the initial stages of putting your vision together (see page 22), this next step will be considerably easier. It's all very well you putting all your subject knowledge, thought and enthusiasm into creating a vision for music, but it won't ever become a reality if you don't get everyone else on board. In a primary school, as we all know, that can be easier said than done.

Just putting your vision statement on the school website or emailing it round to everyone, is probably not going to make the impact you need to get everyone on board with your vision. Instead, you may need to do a bit of legwork to win over hearts and minds!

Communicating your vision to staff

A staff meeting would be the ideal opportunity to introduce your vision. Generally you are unlikely to encounter much argument from teachers as to the necessity of the music curriculum, however, make sure you stress how music can support what they are already doing with reference to the SIP and benefits to children. (If you are based in England, you might also mention that music could be chosen for a deep dive subject inspection next time Ofsted comes to visit.)

Where things might be tricker is with the extra-curricular provision you are providing, particularly if that is in the form of instrumental lessons that children have to leave lessons for! There is no getting round the fact that having children leave in the middle of lessons is disruptive – and instrumental teachers suffer from this too with reading interventions often happening in the middle of whole class music lessons. It is important that you communicate to staff how the extra-curricular programmes you provide are beneficial to children, again linking back to the SIP where necessary, in order to avoid irritation and bad feeling when these disrupt lessons.

Communicating your vision to children

Of course, children don't really have any choice about getting 'on board' with curriculum lessons, but with extra-curricular activities they have to make an additional commitment. Emphasising all the fun performances and activities that they can get involved in (rather than the learning benefits) is a sure fire way to get children to sign up to clubs, ensembles and instrumental lessons, and it is then up to the teacher running these to maintain children's enthusiasm through the 'I want to quit' phase when they realise that they've given up their lunchtime, or that it is a bit harder work than they thought it was going to be!

Try these communication strategies regularly, to ensure that all your children know what is on offer musically at school:

- **a music noticeboard in a prominent position**
- **performances from extra-curricular groups in assembly**
- **a music page on the school website**
- **announcements in assembly about group and individual achievements such as graded exams**

Communicating your vision to parents/carers

We all know that at primary age, children's biggest influence is their parents, so it is crucial that parents know what musical activities are on offer in order to encourage their children to participate. You will also want to outline the benefits of each activity so that parents can make an informed decision about which activities would suit their child.

Rather than just sending a letter saying 'your child can join the choir this term', include information as to why that would be a good idea, in terms of the skills that they will develop. You might also like to talk to class teachers about which children might benefit most from a confidence-boost, an activity that encourages perseverance, or an opportunity to feel 'talented' when perhaps they don't in the classroom, and then talk to their parents about the benefits for that specific child. Do be mindful, however, that if your extra-curricular activities require a financial contribution, this needs to be approached sensitively, as you do not want parents to feel that their child is missing out on important opportunities due to their family financial situation (see *Making it inclusive*, Chapter 7, page 71).

Letters from school can easily get mislaid or forgotten about, so you will want to utilise a range of communication strategies with parents including:

- **a music page on the school website**
- **performances from extra-curricular groups at events to which parents are invited**
- **text alerts when places become available in groups or for instrumental lessons**
- **posts about music activities on your school social media accounts**

Top tip

If this is all sounding like a mammoth task, remember: if you get everyone on board with your vision at the start, that will avoid it all falling apart later down the line! Always remember why you are doing what you are doing.

Chapter 3

Designing your curriculum – practical considerations

In this chapter you will learn how to ensure that your curriculum meets your school's needs, whether you are designing it from scratch or using a bought-in scheme.

- **Getting started**
  - Designing a curriculum from scratch
  - Using a bought-in scheme

- **What to include**
  - Reflecting your school community
  - Decolonising the curriculum and 'cultural capital'

- **Planning for learning**

- **Topic-based learning**

Getting started

3

"We can often see whole KS2 and KS3 music curricula founded solely on the *what* of lesson planning, in other words on what the children and young people will do. Much harder, but much more profitable in the long term, is to start with *why*. 〟 Fautley

When setting out to design or revise your existing curriculum, you need to closely consult your vision statement. The curriculum is the filling in your three I's sandwich and implementing it will take you from your outlined *intent* to your proposed *impact*.

> **Intent**
> The 'big picture' of music in your school – what it is for and how it will benefit your children, including how it contributes to the School Improvement Plan.

> **Implementation**
> How you will achieve what you intend – what activities and resources will be available.

> **Impact**
> What children will be able to do when they leave your school – often best expressed as bullet points.

Most subject leaders will inherit a curriculum and therefore your job at this point may well be to look at what you currently do and whether that will achieve your intended impact. During this latter process, you will also need to take account of *why* your school does what it does in terms of curriculum; there may be additional reasons why certain instruments are always used, or certain topics have been chosen, and sweeping these away to make way for your new vision might cause some upset!

If you are not sticking with your existing curriculum, then you have two options: designing something completely new from scratch, or buying in a scheme (or schemes) to function as your curriculum.

Top tip

Remember though, as with any major project, you should plan backwards from your outcomes rather than forwards towards them. This eliminates the risk of getting to the end of your Year 6 plan and discovering that the children won't be able to do everything you had set out in your impact section.

Designing a curriculum from scratch

Designing a curriculum from scratch will be a time-intensive, laborious but ultimately more satisfying process as you will have full control over all the content so that it meets the outcomes that you have set out.

You will be able to start with your vision and tailor all of your curriculum content and resources to deliver it, rather than having to compromise to the content already prescribed by a particular scheme. You can use the information in the rest of this chapter and those that follow to guide you through the process of designing your curriculum.

Using a bought-in scheme

This might sound like the answer to all your prayers and a good enough reason to stop reading this book immediately! Having all your lesson plans, resources and teaching materials in one place, carefully packaged to be easy to navigate, and designed to ensure progress towards age-related expectations, makes these schemes extremely beneficial for schools, particularly those where music has not traditionally been a 'strong point'. However, you will want to be careful how these schemes are used in your school long term.

As a starting point to 'get music happening', the 'plug and play' approach to using these schemes is the lesser of two ills. However, as Janet Mills points out, this is ultimately a limited and limiting way to teach: "The problem arises when teachers do not think through why they are teaching a particular lesson, in terms of what the students are intended to learn... A lesson that was written for another class in another school will not necessarily work well elsewhere."

The key to using these resources effectively is to get everyone beyond the 'plug and play' stage and into the engagement stage where they actively participate in the 'teaching' of the scheme. Teachers need to be encouraged to read the accompanying lesson plans so they know why they are doing what they are doing, and as they become more confident, to adapt and alter the lessons where necessary so that they suit their own pupils better.

If your school is buying in a fully-resourced curriculum, your first job should be to dig around and find out what curriculum documentation already comes with it. Many subject leaders spend hours creating progression maps and curriculum plans for existing schemes only to discover that these were provided all along but carefully hidden on some obscure part of the publisher's website!

What to include

The next consideration is *what* to include in your curriculum. Whether using a bought-in scheme or adapting/devising your own, at this point it is prudent to remember that most schools are required to follow some form of prescribed national curriculum. As noted in Chapter 1 (see page 8), these usually require children to listen to, perform (singing and with instruments), improvise and compose music, and also gain some theoretical understanding around the way music functions, its place in history, and its communication systems (for example, staff notation). Sometimes particular content is prescribed, but more often than not it is up to subject leaders to choose the content which provides their children the opportunity to get better in all musical skill areas.

Choosing content for your curriculum is the fun part, but it is important not to get too carried away without considering the resources that you have available (or can purchase) for music, and the confidence and competence of your staff to teach various musical concepts (see Chapter 6, page 57). You may find you end up with an ambitious plan A list of content which has to be scaled back, at least in the beginning, into something more manageable. That is OK – curriculum design is a continuous process, and over time you will be able to work towards delivering your "curriculum of dreams". (Stafford)

When considering the content of your curriculum, it is also important to consider the amount of time you have available for the teaching of music. For example, in its 2021 subject research review for music, the English schools' inspectorate, Ofsted, identified that most primary children will only have 15–20 hours a year of music teaching. Consequently, you will need to make hard decisions about what to include, planning for "curriculum content that might reasonably be mastered in the time available, remembering that sometimes less is more". (Ofsted, 2021)

Model Music Curriculum

Teachers in England should be aware that in 2021 the DfE released a Model Music Curriculum, designed to exemplify one possible approach to teaching the national curriculum. This non-statutory document is not compulsory for schools to use, but stands as a guide for the sort of content that might be covered in order to meet the requirements of the national curriculum.

Top tip

When you're choosing content for your curriculum, remember to continually refer back to the 'why' question, the 'impact' section of your vision statement. It is easy to get carried away with all the amazing different topics we could cover, but if the content of your curriculum is not contributing to the aims of your overall music vision, then it needs to change.

At this point you will find it useful to carry out an audit of the resources you already have in school, for example:

- untuned percussion instruments
- tuned instruments
- sheet music and songbooks
- backing tracks
- CDs and videos
- streaming subscriptions
- speakers and sound systems
- manuscript (staff notation) paper and whiteboards
- music reference books

Reflecting your school community

Another consideration when choosing content for your curriculum is the cultural make-up of your school community. Schools should reflect the communities that they serve, and this should be a consideration for incorporating particular musical styles, genres and traditions into your curriculum.

This is not just some trendy idea to make your school look progressive, but in fact an important strategy for getting children on board with formal music education. It refers just as much to the forms of popular music that children listen to at home as it does to the musical traditions of diverse cultures. We need to remember that music is an important component of children and young people's sense of self-identity, and that the music that they listen to outside of the classroom is likely to be much more sophisticated than the music that they can produce themselves in lessons. Ignoring children's 'own' music in our curriculum can alienate them from it, particularly in the upper end of KS2.

> "Where [classroom music activity] is not coupled in the mind of any student with the impact of actual music-making and music-taking relating to experience outside of school, the effect can be of a curriculum which resembles the scraps under a rich man's table, the cold left-overs of other people's meals, often unappetizing. **77** Swanwick

Decolonising the curriculum and 'cultural capital'

There is a tradition across most of the Western world of prioritising our own music, particularly classical music, over and above the music from other parts of the world when we are teaching children about music. You will often hear people describe classical music as 'the highest' or 'the best' form of music, and even government ministers here in the UK have expressed the opinion that children 'should' be (force-) fed a diet of classical music to somehow better themselves.

In England, the concept of 'cultural capital', linked to Ofsted's *inspection framework*, has unwittingly reinforced this message as it makes the point that teachers should be introducing children to "the best that has been thought and said" (Ofsted *School Inspection Handbook*) and teachers default to classical music because they have been told or assumed it represents 'the best'. However, comparing European classical music to Indian classical music, or American pop to Indonesian gamelan music, is like comparing Dickens to Hugo, Cervantes to Shakespeare; these are not like-for-like comparisons as they use completely different languages.

Top tip

When planning for cultural capital, you will want to consider all of the different musical traditions that you would like your children to experience, both reflecting and broadening out from the school community, and find the 'best' examples of these to share. This will then place all the music you study on an equal footing, rather than perpetuating the colonial notion that the conquering white man's music is 'better' than everyone else's!

Planning for learning

Another consideration when planning content for your curriculum is what Professor Martin Fautley describes as "the difference between planning for *doing* and planning for *learning*".

We need to ensure that the content that we select meets our learning aims, in effect moving beyond the idea that 'Children are learning to play *Mary Had a Little Lamb'*, to: 'Children are learning how to hold a glockenspiel beater/play in time/produce a clear sound/read stepwise melodies from staff notation' – or whatever the actual learning intent might be.

This might sound obvious, but often in music we default to 'learning the material' (planning for doing) as our prime purpose, rather than considering the particular musical skills that are being developed through the learning of the material (planning for learning).

Reading recommendation

To get a good overview of the research behind successful curriculum design in music, read Martin Fautley's 'Curriculum Planning & Classroom Music' in *Primary Music Magazine 3.1.*

Reading recommendation

Music in the Early Years is part of a wider holistic approach to learning, and your EYFS colleagues are unlikely to be teaching 'a music lesson' but rather using music activities as part of thematic learning based on the children's interests. You may find *Collins Primary Music – Early Years Foundation Stage* a helpful guide as to how to plan for musical learning within the context of the EYFS.

Topic-based learning

If there is one thing that is guaranteed to derail the careful planning of musical progression, it is topic-based learning! Of course, learning through topics is great, and definitely to be encouraged, but often it results in music being used to support the topic rather than the other way round. While schools are very good at ensuring logical progress of skills and understanding for subjects like English through topic-based work, music can often get relegated to 'sing a topic song'.

As Mary Myatt points out, intervention often needs to occur before the topics are settled on, rather than after the fact otherwise: "They devolve into ridiculous, tenuous links ... a history teacher, desperate to link the theme of colour, including a topic on the Black Death. Or a theme on water, where in religious education this gets translated into Jesus walking on water..." This kind of approach is all too familiar in music, where teachers are reduced to learning 'that song' by the Bangles to fit with 'Ancient Egypt', or singing along to *Greensleeves* for 'The Tudors' because Henry VIII may or may not have written it! As Myatt goes on to say, this results in "the integrity of subjects being degraded".

Top tip

Whether you are planning your own music curriculum within a pre-designed topic-based structure, or selecting units from a pre-existing scheme, then it is really important that you factor in the overall progression of skills in all areas of the music curriculum, rather than just grasping for the nearest song that happens to be about 'The Romans'...

The ideal scenario would be for you to have input into which cross-curricular topics are chosen, so that you can head off any problems from the start.

Chapter 4

Designing your curriculum – musical development

Having considered the *why* and *what* of your curriculum, in this chapter you will think about *how* you are going to deliver it by considering how children develop and progress in music.

- **Taking an holistic approach**

- **Constructing a spiral curriculum**

- **Types of musical knowledge**

- **Models of musical development**

- **Whole class instrumental programmes**

Taking an holistic approach

"**Music Teaching promotes an holistic approach to musical experience which recognises that the richest musical and learning experiences are those where performing, composing, listening and appraising are brought together and the artificial boundaries between composer, performer and listener broken down.** Spruce

Although music can be thought of as an umbrella term for a set of different areas – performing, improvising, composing, listening and building theoretical understanding – it is important not to compartmentalise. All of these skills are in fact interrelated, and children develop better and more reliably across all skill sets when they are taught holistically. What this means in practice is that your curriculum shouldn't be split into 'performance units', 'composing units' and so on, but instead that each individual unit or topic should seek to develop all of these skills alongside each other.

Example

In a KS2 topic about the Blues you might listen to some of the top blues artists (cultural capital!), learn to play a 12-bar blues chord pattern, learn to improvise with the blues scale, and compose your own blues song following the conventions of the style that you have learnt about. You could also incorporate staff notation into these activities if your teachers are confident to do so.

Constructing a spiral curriculum

The idea of a spiral curriculum is well-established in music with a history dating back at least 60 years, and brought to particular prominence by the work of Keith Swanwick and June Tillman. Its basic principle is that over time we revisit "topics, subjects or themes" (Harden and Stamper) to deepen children's understanding. This is because of the nature of progression in music, which can be linear (simple to complex) but can also involve breadth (applying learnt concepts to a range of new contexts), and depth (becoming more 'musical'). More on this in the assessment chapter (see page 47).

As Harden and Stamper note, in a spiral curriculum:

- **Topics [themes or subjects] are revisited**
- **There are increasing levels of difficulty**
- **New learning is related to previous learning**
- **The competence of students increases**

As primary music leader, you will need to decide what the core concepts to be returned to in your spiral curriculum are. For example, they might be:

- the elements of music – which are returned to each year in greater depth and across a greater breadth of musical styles
- the areas of performing, improvising, composing, listening and building theoretical understanding – although do take care that this does not result in an unholistic approach to the curriculum (see page 37)
- key musical styles, genres or traditions that you want children to re-experience over time – this might feel like narrowing the breadth of the curriculum, but it will increase its depth and support linear progress too, which may be a good enough payoff to want to take this approach

Example

If using the elements of music as the core of your spiral curriculum you might take 'duration' and for its first iteration work on pulse, then on rhythm, then on repeated rhythmic features (ostinato, loop, riff, motif), and then on reading and using rhythmic notation.

Types of musical knowledge

In recent years there has been an increasing trend across America and England for the adoption of a 'knowledge-rich' approach to all aspects of the curriculum. At its most reductive, this can result in progress being shown by the *facts* that children can recall, which of course is of limited value in music. However, there are in fact many different types of knowledge, some of which – such as 'procedural' – are essentially just practical skills repackaged!

In music, we have recognised for decades that there are different types of knowledge in our subject. Although there are many different models and theories of musical knowledge, these can be distilled into three broad categories:

• knowledge *about* music
• knowledge *how* to music
• knowledge *of* music

Type of musical knowledge	Definition	Example	Knowledge-rich equivalent
Knowledge **about** music	Facts about music	Lord Kitchener was a calypso musician	Declarative knowledge
Knowledge **how** to music	Skills of making music	I can play five notes on the piano	Procedural knowledge
Knowledge **of** music	Relationship with music	Music makes me feel...	Tacit knowledge*

*Although knowledge of music links to tacit knowledge, it extends beyond this.

When cross-referencing these types of musical knowledge with the content of the national curriculum in whichever country you teach, hopefully you will find that there is a lot more use for knowledge *how* (procedural) than there is for knowledge *about* (declarative)! However, the most important form of musical knowledge is knowledge *of*, as this is what deepens our relationship with music, provides us with rich musical experiences, and keeps us coming back to musical activities throughout our lives.

Example

In a topic on Beethoven, children might learn the number of symphonies that he wrote (knowledge about), how to sing the tune to *Ode to Joy* (knowledge how), and perform this alongside an orchestra and choir in a children's concert, having the experience of being on stage and surrounded by the music (knowledge of).

Top tip

When planning your curriculum you should start with knowledge *of,* thinking about the experiences you want the children to have (linking to your vision), and then working out what knowledge *how* and *about* they will need in order to access these experiences.

Models of musical development

When designing your curriculum, one of the most important/ overarching aims is to help children make progress in music. In order to do that we have discussed on the previous few pages setting up a spiral curriculum which is holistic and provides opportunities to develop the three types of musical knowledge (knowledge *about*, knowledge *how* and knowledge *of*).

What you also need to take into consideration is what is currently known about how children develop across each of the different skill areas of music. The next few pages draw on key research identifying features of musical development in the following: composing, improvising, singing, notation and listening.

Some of the models of musical development that follow are based on age abilities; others present stages that children progress through on their learning journey regardless of age. Although all different, the majority of them show a common theme of beginning with exploration of sound materials, to developing an understanding of how music works, to then challenging these musical 'norms' and the children developing their own individual musical identity.

All of the models provide food for thought for a primary music leader embarking on the process of curriculum design with musical progression in mind. They may help you to decide what kind of activities happen when, and which content you programme in each different year group. They will also help you to reassure your colleagues about what to expect their classes to be able to do, so that they don't beat themselves up with unrealistic expectations!

Composing

The sequence of musical development (Swanwick and Tillman)

In this cumulative model, at primary level children build upon and progress through the following phases:

- **Ages 0–4 ("Material phase")** – children will explore how sounds can be made with their voices and instruments, and may be fascinated by sound quality, especially the extremes of sound. Their compositions are often 'rambling'!

- **Ages 4–9 ("Expressive phase")** – children will use sound for expressive effect, with a particular tendency to use speed and dynamics. They start the phase with little structural control but by age 7/8 they will start to use more conventional phrase structures.

- **Ages 10–15 ("Form phase")** – children will now have a firm grasp of what music is *meant* to sound like, meaning that they can break those rules. There is a focus on repetition, transformation and contrast, and a growing control of technical, expressive and structural features.

2 Improvising

Growing with improvisation (Kratus, 1991)

In this model, there are seven levels of behaviours which are not explicitly tied to age ranges. Instead they represent the levels children progress through as they gain more experience of improvisation. In a typical primary curriculum context, it is likely that you will mainly be focusing on the first three levels.

1. **"Exploration"** – trying out combinations of sound within a loose structure.

2. **"Process-oriented improvisation"** – creating more organised patterns of sound.

3. **"Product-oriented improvisation"** – showing awareness of structural features within an improvisation, for example the use of repeated rhythm.

4. **"Fluid improvisation"** – becoming more fluent in improvising, more automatic with less obvious 'thought' needing to be used.

5. **"Structural improvisation"** – able to give an improvisation an overall structure.

6. **"Stylistic improvisation"** – able to improvise authentically within a particular musical style.

7. **"Personal improvisation"** – able to put their own unique personal stamp onto the improvisation.

3 Singing

Singing and vocal development (Welch)

This model describes how children develop both technically in singing but also in terms of their learning and creating of song material.

- **Ages 0–2** – "babbling" leads into singing "partial songs", often repetitively; some of the pitches are correct and the overall shape of the melody goes up and down in the right places, but the rhythm may be inconsistent, and the key may change throughout.

Singing continued

- **Ages 2–4** – "pot pourri" approach to songs, where existing songs are borrowed and added to children's own creations. Melodic contour (the overall shape of the melody) becomes more recognisable and rhythms more consistent.

- **Ages 4–8** – new songs learnt in the order: "words, rhythm, melodic contour, specific intervals". Tuning becomes more stable and their own songs start to reflect the music that they are familiar with, for example using structural features such as a chorus.

- **Ages 8–11** – finer control of dynamics and rhythm, and sustained singing over longer phrases. Most children are able to sing in tune by age 11 (though boys lag behind girls).

Notation

The mind behind the musical ear (Bamberger)

This model deals with how children naturally start to try to notate music and how their graphic representation shows musical understanding. What is really interesting about this research is that while many schools use graphic notation as a preparation for and introduction to learning staff notation, this model shows that there is in fact no link between these two forms of notation in terms of musical development – the two are separate developmentally and have no impact on each other so cannot be linked as progression!

- **Type O** – rhythmic scribbles which correspond to the movement of the music.

- **Type F (Figural)** – graphic representations organised by the shapes within the music.

- **Type M (Metric)** – graphic representations organised by the division of time within the music*.

- **Formal staff notation** – there is no natural developmental process that results in you learning staff notation, you have to be taught it: "a result of tuition rather than intuition".

*Type F and Type M can happen interchangeably at the same time.

5 Listening

These models are particularly helpful for devising appropriate questions and activities in response to the music that you are listening to with your class. They will also help you to select your listening material in the first place, choosing pieces with features that your children will naturally recognise at a certain stage in their development.

Making Sense of Music (Durant and Welch, 1995)

- **Ages 4–6 ("Personal Expressiveness")** – aware of the expressive qualities of music, and able to express these by comparing them to characters, moods and stories.

- **Ages 7–8 ("Vernacular")** – can recognise "established musical conventions".

- **Ages 9–11 ("Speculative")** – able to recognise deviations from the norm, and able to describe how expressive effects are created with musical devices.

Musical Identities Mediate Musical Development (Hargreaves, MacDonald and Miell, 2006)

There is a 'dip' in open-earedness (willingness to listen to different types of music) in later childhood which occurs at around the age of 10 or 11 years which typically shows itself in strong preferences for a narrow range of pop styles, and strong general dislike for all other styles.

Whole class instrumental programmes

In England, whole class instrumental programmes (often known as wider opportunities, first access, WCET...) have been around for almost two decades now, and they are also becoming increasingly used in other parts of the UK, and beyond. They either involve the whole class learning one instrument (with some of the most popular options being ukulele, recorder, and trumpet) or learning in an ensemble set-up where the class may be divided onto different instruments to make a mini brass or wind band, or string orchestra.

Initially, when these were rolled out, people got very tangled up in the 'instrumental' aspect of these, and there was a lot of pushback from instrumental teachers about how these programmes would 'never' work because one teacher working with 30 children could not help them achieve the same technical standard as in the standard set-ups of small group or one-to-one instrumental tuition. This of course, was a fallacy born of the misunderstanding that the main focus of these programmes was the 'instrumental' aspect – unsurprising since even when these were branded as 'wider opportunities' they were almost always referred to by teachers and children as, for example, 'the trumpet lesson'!

Whole class instrumental programmes were never intended to replace the curriculum, but instead to run alongside it as an additional music lesson. For fairly obvious reasons, it is rare to find schools adopting this originally intended structure, and instead providers ensure that the national curriculum is covered within the whole class instrumental programme.

A lot of developmental and research work has occurred on these programmes since the pilot phase in 2003, and our understanding of how these programmes work best has refined. Essentially, these programmes are a 'music lesson taught through an instrument' (or family of instruments), rather than an 'instrumental lesson'. This is great news for your curriculum planning because it means that if you are replacing a term or a year of curriculum music with a whole class instrumental programme, this should not affect your progression plan.

Top tip

Remember that if you are planning a whole class instrumental programme at some point in your children's musical learning journey, the key thing is to make sure that you treat this as part of your curriculum. This is particularly important if your programme is being delivered by an external specialist; they should work with you to deliver a programme which fits into the 'gap' in your curriculum and achieves the aims that you have set out for that year group.

When to plan for the year of instrumental teaching

The main progression issue you may have around whole class instrumental is in fact how you progress on from it afterwards. The original 'wider opportunities' programmes in England were aimed at Year 4, but for a long time now there has been no formal requirement for them to happen in a particular year group. This is great news for schools where the only 'specialist' music teacher is the visiting instrumental teacher, as it means that you can schedule your whole class programmes at the apex of your curriculum. In this scenario it makes much more sense for the 'specialist' teaching to take place in Year 6 (or perhaps more realistically Year 5, as sadly there may be limited time in Year 6 for music!) rather than having it happen in Year 4 and then expecting a non-specialist class teacher to be able to extend children's musical learning the following year.

Many providers will come with their own fixed 'scheme' that they wish to use, but your job as music subject leader is to ensure the quality of and progression within the curriculum, so don't be afraid to ask them to work with you to create a scheme which works for both of you. After all, it is the school not the external provider who are held accountable for the quality of the curriculum. The reading recommendation will give you a framework in which to have these discussions and build connections between the work of the specialist and the school's overall music curriculum.

Reading recommendation

Music Education Solutions® on behalf of Sky music hub carried out a long-term research project on whole class instrumental teaching which culminated in the publication of the Sky music hub's *WCET Best Practice Project*. This document provides a research review and various tools to help you deliver outstanding whole class provision in your school (**skymusichub.com/the-hub/downloads**).

How to teach Whole-class instrumental lessons by Kay Charlton offers loads of great ideas, support and advice for whole-class instrumental teaching.

Chapter 5

Designing your curriculum – assessment

Assessment in music is a thorny issue even before you take statutory requirements into consideration! There are both philosophical and practical reasons why assessing progress in music is very different from assessment in, for example, maths or English. This chapter will help you think about what it is that you're assessing, and why you're assessing it.

- **Philosophy of assessment**

- **Practicalities of assessment**
    - Informal assessment
    - Formal assessment

- **Purpose of assessment**

- **What to assess**
    - Assessing via key skill areas
    - Assessing via musical elements
    - Assessing via knowledge acquired

- **Formalising your assessment strategy**

Philosophy of assessment

"[Assessment] is made all the more difficult in music education because there are different types of musical thinking and musical knowledge that teachers wish pupils to engage with... Thus a complex construct like musical ability does not have a single unitary outcome; we do not say that a pupil has a musical ability of 45%, for example, as this would be meaningless. **"** Fautley, 2010

Assessment is problematic in music for two main reasons:

1. Music is actually an umbrella category for lots of different related skills:

- performing music – using both voices and a range of instruments which may all require different techniques
- listening to music – which requires identifying musical details and discussing the rationale for these using musical vocabulary
- improvising – where children synthesise the music around them to create instant responses
- composing – which requires children to create and refine music to be fit for a specific purpose
- building theoretical understanding – about notation (requiring decoding and fluency in reading) and the history of music (which may result in a 'knowledge bank' that needs to be learnt if your school takes a knowledge-rich approach)

As teachers, we would all agree that it would not be fair to 'mark down' a brilliant pianist just because they happened to be awful at playing the flute, but the alternative is to provide a separate assessment for each different musical skill, which in a primary classroom context would be time-consuming and, one might suggest, overkill. We need to find a balance between capturing all that our children can and cannot yet do so that we can celebrate and support them, with the reality of the time teachers have available to formally record assessment.

2. Progress in music, even when broken down into all its separate skill areas, is not necessarily linear

While we might be used to showing progression in other areas of the curriculum as steady progress through harder and more complex concepts, in music there is the possibility to get 'better' at simple tasks. We might even say that being able to do simple things 'better' is more valuable than being able to do complicated things badly, as it shows a greater depth of musicianship. When you also add in the factor of breadth of knowledge – applying your existing musical skills across a range of styles and traditions – it becomes apparent that plotting progress on a linear pathway is not going to be representative of what our children can actually do.

"**Performing a wide range of complex music without evidence of understanding would definitely not count as a high level of achievement. And it is certainly possible to perform, compose and enjoy a high-quality musical experience without any great complexity.** Swanwick, 2012

Reading recommendation

Professor Martin Fautley is world-renowned for his work on assessment in music education. He has published several books on the subject, and his articles can be found in all the major music education journals. He also publishes a blog which is a great starting point for subject leaders to get to know his work (**drfautley.wordpress.com**).

Practicalities of assessment

In other subjects, formal assessment can be pretty straightforward, and probably consists of collecting in workbooks and marking them. Not so for music! Unless you are going to video your entire lesson every week and then take the footage home to scrutinise afterwards (please don't do that to yourself!) then you're going to have to pick your moments when it comes to formal assessment of your children's musical progress.

Informal assessment

It is important to remember that not all assessment needs to be formalised, and that teachers are constantly assessing during lessons without even thinking about it. Instant intervention as and when children need it is going to be far more useful than making a note of what they can't do and then trying to address it afterwards.

Top tip

For music, formative assessment for learning is much more valuable 'in the moment' than delivered after the fact.

Formal assessment

That said, you will want a 'formal' record of children's achievement at some point so that you can use it for your planning moving forward. Aside from noting on your planning any children who might need support next lesson, the end of a unit or topic can often provide an opportunity for more extensive formal assessment.

Video a final performance of whatever you have been working on, and use this to help you plan the next topic, but also show it to the children so they can critique their own work. Over time you will have a bank of recordings that you can compare to show progress, which will be useful for SLT, Ofsted, and to show children how far they have come.

Top tip

You can learn much from EYFS colleagues as the strategies they use for capturing learning, which at this stage is often not literacy based and cannot be 'marked', translate perfectly onto practical subjects like music. Taking photographs, video clips, and writing quick notes on post-its or observation forms are all great ways to capture progress or difficulties in practical music making.

Purpose of assessment

Before you go about creating an assessment strategy for music, it is important to consider why you are actually carrying out the assessment in the first place.

Since a lot of the assessment work that helps children to improve does not require formalising, and is better delivered 'in the moment' (see *Practicalities of assessment*, page 50), where more formal assessment methods have value in supporting pupil progress is as an aide-memoire for the teacher so that they know who to support and what to plan for in the next lesson or unit, or as a tool for self-assessment, such as watching back a video of a performance.

Given that the majority of the assessment that you 'do' for children and for your own planning will be less formal, it follows that if you are doing more formal assessment on top of this, and particularly if that involves creating sets of data, you must be doing it for someone else! It is important to remember that data sets have very limited impact on learning, and (if you are in England) that Ofsted no longer looks at internal data. If you are being asked by your SLT to plot progress on a graph, or give children 'levels' in music, then it is reasonable to ask them why this is required!

Top tip

What Ofsted are, and your SLT should be, interested in is assessment evidence rather than data. So when you go about designing the assessments that form part of your music curriculum, the focus should be on the collection of evidence such as video and audio files, electronic files for any music technology work, and any written work that you might possibly have for staff notation or history of music. This will enable you to 'prove' progress over time, which is the whole point of this additional type of assessment.

What to assess

In music, 'what' you are assessing could be almost anything (see *Philosophy of assessment,* page 48), so you will want to identify the key things that you wish to know about pupil progress over time.

Assessing via key skill areas

For many schools the simplest answer will be to design assessments which show progress over time in the areas of performing, listening, improvising and composing, and in the building of theoretical understanding, for example:

• sing a certain range of notes with accuracy

• maintain a steady beat on a drum

• recognise dynamic changes when listening to music

• use a beginning – middle – end structure in a composition

This strategy is definitely the clearest and easiest to understand, but it does slightly undermine the message of constructing a curriculum where all of these skills are interwoven holistically! On a practical level though, it will provide an easy tick list, and some useful information about which children need help in which skill area during the next topic or unit.

Assessing via musical elements

Other schools may wish to focus their assessment around the elements of music and the processes of recognising, understanding and using these over time. For each child you would identify whether they can:

• recognise each of the elements when they hear them

• understand what each term means so that they can describe what they are hearing using musical vocabulary

• use these in performance and to what extent (can they just do loud and quiet, or can they give you subtle changes of dynamic)

• put them to creative use in composing activities

It needs noting that this in itself may not be a linear process, and many children will of course be able to recognise, perform and compose with the elements of music without knowing what they are called or being able to define them in musical terms.

Assessing via knowledge acquired

If your school is adopting a 'knowledge-rich' approach to the curriculum, then you may have to centre your assessment process around the 'knowledge' that children have acquired. This may involve the use of end of unit quizzes and knowledge catchers. However, it is important to remember that these only capture one very specific type of knowledge – declarative knowledge or knowledge 'about' music, which demonstrates what facts children have memorised. You will also want to show how children have progressed in their skills-based procedural knowledge 'how,' and in their knowledge 'of' music, as these latter two types of knowledge are more important in music than the recall of facts (see *Types of musical knowledge,* page 39).

Formalising your assessment strategy

By now you may have a clear idea of how and when you expect assessment to be carried out during the course of the school year. At this point it is crucial that this information is woven into your curriculum in your medium-term planning, rather than presented as a stand-alone assessment strategy.

This is because teachers are time poor, and they are most likely going to default to just reading the medium-term plan and delivering the lesson without cross-referencing the assessment strategy.

Top tip

Ensure that your curriculum documentation contains informal assessment for learning assessment prompts, and that once in a while there is a more formalised 'assessment lesson' within your curriculum. Then it is far more likely that teachers will remember to collect the evidence that you need.

Chapter 6

Supporting your colleagues with music

In this chapter you will learn how to take a supportive approach to developing your colleagues' confidence and skill in teaching music.

- **Developing colleagues' confidence**
  - Using commercial schemes of work to boost staff confidence

- **Developing colleagues' musical understanding and skill**
  - Identifying staff skill priorities

- **Delivering your action plan**

- **Helping colleagues to differentiate their teaching**
  - Differentiation by support and through feedback
  - Differentiation by task or resource
  - Differentiation through stretch and challenge
  - Differentiation for SEND

Developing colleagues' confidence

It might be a slight exaggeration to say that all of the problems with music in primary schools come down to teacher confidence, but it is not far off! As you will know from your own experience of teacher training, it is rare for more than a few hours of attention to be paid to music across the life of the course. This is then compounded by the fact that it is comparatively rare to be able to observe (and teach) music during a teaching placement, since the teachers you are working with have all come through the same system which leaves them less likely to want to demonstrate a music lesson to you, due to lack of confidence in their own ability. And so the cycle continues...!

But it is not just a lack of training that causes a lack of confidence in primary teachers; the problem goes deeper than that, right back to their own school days. Across most of the Western world, we adopt a philosophy of 'talent' being the key to 'musicianship'. By giving some children additional lessons on instruments, by holding auditions for choirs and ensembles, by handing out certificates in assemblies and selecting certain children to perform as 'soloists', we can unintentionally give the impression that music is only for 'special' or 'talented' children, and everyone else is 'unmusical'. These kinds of special, elective activities traditionally (though things are getting better in the present day) require the learning of staff notation, which places another barrier between the 'musical' and 'unmusical' children.

Top tip

Whilst as a primary music leader you don't have control over what initial teacher training experience your colleagues have with music, if you do have trainees in your school it would be worth liaising with the school-based teacher training mentor to try to arrange some music observation and even teaching opportunities for them, as they are unlikely to be getting meaningful input into this elsewhere.

Teachers who have grown up through this system will often therefore identify themselves as 'unmusical' purely on the basis that they do not play an instrument or read music, and by and large their experience of teacher training will only reinforce this, since the lack of attention given to music in many teacher training courses may give the subconscious impression that teachers 'should' already be able to 'do' music.

Top tip

When dealing with teacher confidence as a subject leader, it may be useful to think about what we would say to a child in the same position. We would never want children to think that they weren't 'talented' or 'good enough' to take part in music, and we would make every effort to encourage and support them. We know that the majority of children are able to achieve against every aspect of the music curriculum, and therefore it logically follows that their teachers, with all those extra years of experience and learning, are capable of that too!

This complex, multi-layered confidence problem cannot be instantly fixed. You can't go on a course or take part in a music staff meeting and magically decide you are 'musical' after all! As a primary music leader it is important to listen to staff articulate *if* and *why* they don't feel confident – often you will find that with some probing you can uncover some misconceptions about what music teaching actually involves, or specific areas of the curriculum that feel like a step too far for some of your teachers.

Top tip

If you are dealing with low levels of confidence among your colleagues, start with listening to music. This requires no specialist musical 'talent' and in fact, if the listener doesn't 'get' what the composer or artist was intending, it could be argued that it is the composer's/artist's fault, not the listener's! Ask your colleagues to share their favourite piece of music and say why they like it – this conversation should help you to draw out the fact that music is for everyone, and that all opinions are valid.

Using commercial schemes of work to boost staff confidence

If a lack of confidence is preventing your colleagues from teaching music, then investing in an all-singing, all-dancing scheme of work designed for non-specialist teachers could be just the ticket. Having a fully-resourced scheme to work from means that teachers don't have to worry about designing their lessons and looking for supporting materials, they simply follow the instructions provided and, as if by magic, they are teaching music!

Top tip

If your school is in England, you may wish to be a little bit careful with how you use schemes of work for music, in case you are subject to a music deep dive during an Ofsted inspection. The inspector will want to establish that teachers know where their lessons are coming from and going to in terms of progression, so you will need to move beyond a model where teachers load up the next lesson, or turn the next page and teach what is prescribed without thinking about the context of the scheme as a whole.

Schemes of work can really help boost teachers' confidence and show them that they *can* teach music, but in the long-term you will want to develop their skills further so that they can use these sorts of schemes more effectively, and even start to create their own lessons and materials to supplement them.

Developing colleagues' musical understanding and skill

Following on from your work with colleagues around their confidence levels with music, the next step will be to carry out a skills audit. This could take a number of forms to suit your own school, but the most logical way to approach this might be to ask each teacher to complete a self-assessment survey based on the contents of the music national curriculum. There is an editable skills audit template online, which you can adapt to suit your individual needs (see online resources).

Identifying staff skill priorities

Once all your colleagues have completed their self-assessment skills audit you will want to turn all this data into a set of priorities which can form the basis of an action plan. If you are lucky, your colleagues will all have identified the same areas for development, which will make the job a lot easier. If all of them say they don't know what the elements of music are, at least you know where to start!

If the responses are more mixed, you will need to make some tough decisions about who and what to prioritise. To do this, you will want to think of the following factors:

- **Quick wins** – what can you fix almost instantly to make an impact on teaching quality?
- **Vision** – which issues will impact most negatively on the delivery of your vision?
- **School improvement** – which issues align most closely to the aims of your SIP?
- **Fundamentals of music** – which basic issues need to be fixed first?
- **Staffing teams** – who will benefit most, and who will they then be able to support in turn?

This will help you to sort the areas for development into priority order, and then you can start at the top of the list this year and work your way down. How many issues you tackle in one year will depend on the time it will take to fix them. For example, teaching everyone the basic definitions of the elements of music and how to recognise them in a piece of music might only take one staff meeting, whereas mentoring someone to become confident to lead singing sessions might take a series of demonstration, team teaching, and observation sessions.

Top tip

The key thing to remember, as always, is that you are only one person, and there is only so much you can do in one year, especially if you also have full-time responsibility for your own class! As long as you have identified all the 'problems' that need fixing, and are working towards solving some of them, then you are on top of your responsibilities as a subject leader.

Delivering your action plan

Once you have established your priority areas for staff development, you can make a plan to address them. The first and most obvious thing to remember is that while music may be your own focus, your colleagues have other commitments and may be leading other subjects themselves, so you can't expect them to make their musical development their sole focus!

You will want to come up with a range of development strategies that will address your priority areas succinctly and efficiently without overloading your colleagues. It is important too that you discuss your proposals with the teachers involved to find out whether they agree that your idea is the best way of providing them with support. If your colleagues feel they are being made to do something that isn't going to have the impact that they want, they are less likely to buy into the whole process, which may mean that you go to a lot of effort for very little return!

Reading recommendation

Published in 2016, the DfE's *Standard for Teachers' Professional Development* guidance is a useful starting point for ensuring that the development opportunities which you provide for your colleagues will be impactful. Find it at: **gov.uk/government/publications/standard-for-teachers-professional-development**

Staff development methods

- Teaching resources with inbuilt CPD
- Lesson observations and feedback
- Video tutorials
- Staff meetings
- Podcasts
- INSET
- Team teaching
- Co-planning
- Books and articles
- External courses and conferences (live and online)
- Demonstration lessons

Helping colleagues to differentiate their teaching

There are many reasons why differentiation in music can be tricky. The first of these is the recognition that differentiation is actually required. Many teachers have themselves grown up in a system where only the 'talented' children excelled at music; they were the special ones who had instrumental lessons, and took part in the choir and the orchestra, while everyone else just played the theme tune to *Titanic* with one finger on the keyboard. As discussed earlier in this chapter, across Western education systems we adopted this 'talent' myth for a long time, meaning that teachers now may assume that you can either 'do' music or you 'can't'. This can result in lessons being taught at one level with no attempt to support children who don't 'get' it. This isn't a criticism of individual teachers or their attitudes, it is just an acknowledgement that they themselves may have felt 'unmusical' at school, and therefore may accept it as the norm that some children will be 'talented' or 'musical' and others won't.

Even when teachers acknowledge the need to differentiate their music lessons, there are still a number of barriers to overcome:

• If teachers are not confident about their own level of musical skill, then it is particularly difficult for them to provide stretch activities for the more able students.

• It may also be difficult for them to help children having difficulty with the activities if they are not sure themselves how to do it either.

• Even if teachers feel confident to 'have a go' at differentiation, any differentiated group work activities can be noisy and chaotic in a way that it wouldn't be for maths or English!

All these factors can add up to a perfect storm where lessons are taught without proper consideration to each child's individual needs.

Differentiation by support and through feedback

The first step on your school's musical differentiation journey is to help staff understand how to give meaningful feedback on musical tasks. This process of 'differentiation by support' is a really effective tool in music, so much so that many years ago when the DfE looked at making changes to how KS3 was delivered, they actually used music as the example of how differentiation by support could encourage learning.

The advantage of differentiation by support for music is that it doesn't involve creating additional tasks which then result in additional noise and chaos in the classroom! It also reinforces the idea that music is for 'everyone', not just the talented few; it sets out the expectation that everyone will be able to achieve the goal of the lesson, but some will need more support to do so. This will have additional, wider benefits beyond music in schools which are adopting a growth mindset approach to learning.

Even teachers who self-identify as 'not musical' will be able to give feedback and support on their children's performances, compositions, and listening and responding activities. After all, everyone knows that it is much easier to be a critic than an artist...! You can encourage your colleagues to use the attainment language from your curriculum as a framework for feedback, such as in the examples below, which take the national curriculum for music in England as an example.

Feedback on performance

- **Accuracy** – Examples: are they playing the right notes? Are they playing in time? Are they following the performance directions (such as dynamics)?

  "That bit didn't sound quite right, did you play a D here, or a different note?"

- **Fluency** – Can they perform the whole piece without hesitation?

  "You had to stop and think about it in the middle; let's practise that bit again."

- **Control** – Are they playing/singing using correct techniques?

  "Remember not to hold your beater like a pencil, hold it in your fist and bounce it gently."

- **Expression** – Have they captured the 'feel' of the piece in their performance?

  "Hmm, I think your singing was a bit angry for a lullaby, we don't want to wake the baby up!"

Feedback on composing

- **Structure** – Does the piece have a clear beginning, middle and end? In KS2, does it have contrasting sections, or follow the formal structure you have asked them to work with?

  "How could you make a greater contrast between the two sections?"

- **Interrelated dimensions** – Does the piece make appropriate use of the interrelated dimensions of music to add interest and special effects?

  "Have you thought about adding some dynamics?"

- **Fit for purpose** – Does the style and construction of the piece reflect the purpose for which it has been written?

  "It's a bit long for a radio jingle!"

Feedback on listening

- **Attention to detail** – How many of the detailed features of the music have they spotted?

  "Are you sure it was fast all the way through?"

- **Depth of answers** – Can they explain why the music sounds the way it does?

  "That's interesting, can you tell me why the composer might have done that?"

- **Musical vocabulary** – Can they use musical vocabulary to describe what's happening in the music?

  "Do you know a musical word for that?"

Differentiation by task or resource

So far we have been talking about differentiation by support and through feedback because that is the most logical and the easiest way to ensure that all of our children's needs are being met in our music lessons. However, sometimes you might need to go further and provide completely different activities for some children – which brings us back to the thorny problem of noise!

Your colleagues may well be put off from the idea of differentiating their lessons because of the potential associated noise. So you may need to think around how you can help them to differentiate by task or resource without losing their minds and irritating everyone else working within 100 metres of their classroom!

Performance activities

For performance activities, there is a growing range of materials on the market with differentiated parts, and some schemes have these integrated into their activities, so that children can play or sing the part that best suits their abilities.

If you don't have the budget for these pre-made resources, you can support your colleagues to identify how parts could be simplified, for example:

Less

- Play the beat on untuned percussion
- Play the rhythm on untuned percussion
- Play one long note each line (unless the harmony changes a lot, in which case that might sound yucky!)
- Play just the first note of each bar
- Sing the melody instead of playing it

More
- Play just a small section (for example, the chorus)

Composing activities

For composing activities, your best friend is space. If you want to truly differentiate the tasks each group is set, then having additional space to spread out into is almost non-negotiable. (And indeed this is useful for any composing task regardless of the differentiation methods employed.)

Once your children are in a space where they can hear their group and not become distracted by the others, you could alter the level of challenge by asking groups to, for example:

- compose a certain number of sections
- use a certain number of instruments
- only use certain notes, depending on the nature of the activity

For example, a group who are struggling might just be asked to compose a short piece in one section which uses a couple of different notes, while a more confident group might have a contrasting section in between two identical sections (ABA), and use a full scale in their piece.

Differentiation through stretch and challenge

Due to the fact that there are many opportunities for children to engage with musical activities outside of the classroom, music is one of the subjects where you are likely to discover that a significant proportion of your children are achieving above expectations. Often these children can complete lesson tasks with ease, and are then given busy work like helping other children if teachers are not sure how to increase the level of challenge in the lesson.

For the most part, the kind of 'gifted and talented' behaviours you are likely to see in music lessons tend to be related to skills learnt in instrumental lessons. Often there is a level of staff notation (or other notation) literacy that is quite far advanced compared to children who have not had instrumental lessons, and a greater range of musical vocabulary is known and understood. They will, of course, also have some facility in playing a 'real' instrument, rather than just the chime bars or tambourine!

Here are some stretch and challenge strategies to suggest your colleagues may use:

Stretch and challenge strategies

Use staff notation	Instead of letter notation that other children may be using, these children could play from staff notation. They could also write elements of their compositions down in staff notation, such as repeating rhythms or simple melodies, but are unlikely to have yet reached the stage where they could write an entire piece out.
Use musical terminology	Instead of using general vocabulary such as 'loud' and 'quiet' you could specifically encourage these children to use the Italian musical terms, such as 'forte' and 'piano' (perhaps using vocabulary lists for older classes if you have created these as part of your curriculum).
Use own instruments	Instead of using classroom percussion, children could bring their own instrument into lessons and use that, provided that they are at the stage where they are confident in how to find a reasonable range of notes without help from their instrumental teacher.
The same, but more!	These children can complete the same activity as the rest of the class, but with additional requirements, for example adding an extra number of sections for a composition.
Lead a group	A slightly more tenuous, but still valuable strategy, is to ask these children to be group leaders, developing their transferrable skills but whilst also helping other children to be involved in a more musical outcome than they would perhaps have had working alone.

Differentiation for SEND

There is, of course, no one-size-fits-all approach to differentiation for special educational needs and disability, because every child is different, so it is important to support your colleagues to find ways to make their music lessons inclusive and accessible to all.

Dr Sarah Mawby identifies seven key principles of effective music activities that serve as good reminders for those of us in mainstream education who may default to giving our SEND children something 'different' to do instead of involving them in the music lesson. These are:

- adapting provision to suit pupil needs
- adapting provision to suit pupil preferences
- knowing the students
- offering musical opportunities
- making it accessible
- making it participatory
- having fun

In the next chapter you will find details of a range of organisations who can provide advice and support for making your music offer more inclusive (see page 71).

Reading recommendation

Dr Sarah Mawby's PhD thesis, 'Music in Schools for Children with Special Educational Needs: A Whole School Perspective' (University of Leeds, 2018), although based on research in special education, has much to teach us about creating meaningful musical experiences for children with special educational needs and disability. Dr Mawby's thesis is available to access freely through White Rose eTheses Online (**etheses.whiterose.ac.uk/24097**)

Chapter 7

Designing your extra-curricular programme

In this chapter you will consider how extra-curricular activities can be used to enhance the musical life of your school.

- **Deciding what extra-curricular activities to provide**

- **Extending the curriculum**

- **Genres, styles and traditions**

- **Performances**

- **Making it inclusive**

Deciding what extra-curricular activities to provide

When choosing what kind of extra-curricular activities to provide, you are going to want to refer back to (you guessed it) your vision for music in your school! Whether you have an existing programme of activities or are starting from scratch, you need to consider how these achieve the aims that you have created.

That said, sometimes starting with a blank slate can be a daunting prospect with just too much choice. If you are looking for some ideas to get you started, then a choir is an obvious choice, as are some instrumental lessons, and of course a weekly 'singing assembly'. Don't be limited to just these choices though, depending on teacher expertise and resources, you could have a range of different instrumental ensembles, a music technology club, a composing club, or even a lunchtime karaoke club!

Key questions

- Which areas of my music vision could be delivered through extra-curricular activities?

- What benefits do our existing extra-curricular activities provide?

- What new activities could we provide to achieve our aims?

- What kind of activities would our children be unable to access unless school provided them?

Top tip

Children in the EYFS are unlikely to access formal extra-curricular activities, but it's important to plan for them to explore their musical side, so keep a box of instruments in the classroom that they can play with during their free activity time.

Extending the curriculum

When it comes to *extra*-curricular activities, you might reasonably think that the whole point of those is that they are nothing to do with the curriculum. There is certainly something to be said for providing a range of enjoyable activities for children that don't feel like yet another 'lesson'. However, with a subject like music, which usually only attracts limited curriculum time and is a practical subject requiring regular practice to embed skills, linking back to the curriculum can be beneficial.

The most obvious example of this can be found in schools where whole class instrumental programmes are followed up with 'continuation' routes; usually small group lessons and/or ensembles. This allows children to embed and extend their instrumental skills, as well as reinforce and develop further their general musical skills.

Key questions

- Which music curriculum areas do our children need more practice with?

- Which curriculum opportunities do they most enjoy?

- Which curriculum activities would benefit from extension with extra-curricular activities?

Genres, styles and traditions

It is crucial to give children an understanding of the multi-cultural society in which we live, and music is one of the best vehicles for this task. Moreover, in the national curriculum for England, and in many other countries' curricula, we are actively encouraged to explore music from a 'wide range' of traditions.

Most schools are really great at including lots of different musical traditions within their curriculum, but often extra-curricular activities default to those that are solely rooted in Western musical genres. This approach undermines our good work in the curriculum in that it positions non-Western musical traditions as 'other' musics, distinct from the musical activities we ourselves are involved in.

"Is our understanding of Western music 'as a universal language' actually an attempt to assimilate our students into 'our' musical culture – albeit with the inclusion of diverse musics and cultural contexts? 🗨 Benedict

As primary music leader, you may wish to consider the range of styles, genres and traditions covered in your extra-curricular provision, and ensure meaningful coverage of non-Western musics. This doesn't just mean ensuring that your choir sings 'African' songs (the term in itself being a homogenisation of a diverse set of countries); the concept of a choir is a Western construct, so careful consideration should be given to repertoire and avoiding cultural misappropriation. You should consider ways to bring authentic musical experiences into your extra-curricular programme using specialist input, whether it be offering a djembe group or a steel pan band, or including sitar and tabla in your instrumental lesson options.

As well as looking for inspiration outside Western traditions for your extra-curricular programme, it is also important to look inwards, to ensure that the Western music we are promoting reflects the interests of our school communities. Music is a crucial part of our children's lives outside school, but often the musical opportunities offered to them in school are not reflective of the music they like to listen to at home. As primary music leader, it is worth considering whether your extra-curricular programme reflects children's own musical interests and allows them to use these to develop their musical learning. You could have a school rock band, a songwriting club, or a rap academy!

Key questions

- Which cultures are represented in my school and what are their musical traditions?

- Which other cultures is it important for my children to learn about?

- Who is available locally to deliver new extra-curricular opportunities?

- What resources will we need, and what will they cost?

- Do children have opportunities to perform and create the sort of music that they would listen to at home?

Performances

When we think of music in primary schools, we probably instantly think of performances, with children singing their hearts out on stage, or perhaps scraping out something unrecognisable on the violin! However proficient the performers, performance events are an integral part of the wider life of the school, and you will want to give all of your pupils the chance to participate in some way.

As primary music leader, you may want to think of your performance schedule strategically, as having a performance to aim for can be a great motivator for children. It's an all too common occurrence when children skip up to you in the corridor to tell you they're 'quitting' a music activity, and often this is because the effort of turning up every week outweighs the reward. Always having a performance to aim for on the not-too distant horizon makes it easier to keep children engaged in extra-curricular activities; 'Oh but if you quit *now*, you'll miss...'

Top tip

Performances can be a great way to showcase musical learning, as well as to help children develop their confidence, and the presentation and communication skills they may need later in life.

Performances are also a great way to attract new recruits for musical activities, so you should aim for a mix of events that are for parents of existing children, but also some taking place within school for other children to watch and be inspired by. You will also want to consider becoming involved in external performances, such as those organised by local music education hubs and community groups.

While performances are great, and definitely to be encouraged, they take a lot of organising, and the job shouldn't solely be left to you just because you are the music subject leader! You will want to approach your school administrators, business manager and site manager for support with the general organisation, so that you can concentrate on making these events fantastic musical experiences for your children. Remember, the history subject lead isn't organising multiple archaeological digs, and the geography subject lead isn't marching children up mountains every half term!

Key questions

- Which performance events do we traditionally provide (for example carol concert, end of year show...)?

- Which times of year do children usually start wanting to 'quit' music activities?

- Are there any seasonal 'gaps' in our performance schedule that need plugging?

- Are there opportunities for children not involved in particular music activities to watch the performances?

- Are there opportunities for all children to participate in a performance?

Making it inclusive

Primary schools are all about inclusivity, and within your extra-curricular strategy you will want to make provision for those children who, for any reason, might not ordinarily be able to take part in musical activities. For example:

- Pupil Premium money can be spent on music in order to make instrumental lessons and extra-curricular activities accessible to low-income families.

- Having an 'all-comers welcome' policy with no 'auditions' will ensure that all children are able to access your extra-curricular provision whatever their level of attainment or experience.

However, access for all is only the first step, and you also need to consider how you will make these activities inclusive for children with additional needs, particularly if they take place at a time when their learning mentor would not ordinarily be working with them. You will need to consider the child's learning and physical needs and plan accordingly so that they are able to meaningfully participate in the activity.

Finally, you might want to consider whether inclusivity stops at the school gate, or whether you want to treat your extra-curricular programme as a community resource. Whether it is partnering with other schools in your cluster or Multi-Academy Trust (MAT) to provide after-school music clubs, or organising and hosting a community choir or band, your school may have a role in providing accessible music-making activities within your local area. Again, this is not a job just for you as primary music leader, but something that your SLT and governors will want to be involved with.

Top tip

The following organisations offer support and advice for inclusive extra-curricular provision:

Jessie's Fund (jessiesfund.org.uk) offers a variety of training packages, including some for instrumental tutors, and for non-music-specialist staff.

Open Up Music (openupmusic.org) offers an 'Open Orchestras' package, which includes adaptive instruments, resources and training, to enable organisations to start an inclusive orchestra.

Drake Music (drakemusic.org) provides one of the most comprehensive offerings of music education delivery from a national provider. They offer individual and whole class instrumental lessons, and also provide a service where they will create a brand new instrument if the children cannot access the instruments on offer.

Chapter 8

Resourcing your curriculum

By far the most fun part of a primary music leader's role is choosing all the resources that you need to deliver your curriculum – provided that your SLT gives you enough budget to buy what you need! This chapter will advise you on how to select the perfect resources to bring your music vision to life.

- **Choosing instruments**

- **Storing and transporting instruments**

- **Music technology**

- **Other useful resources**

- **Copyright and licensing**

Choosing instruments

When choosing your instruments, be mindful of the fact that one set of instruments is not going to cover the curriculum requirements for EYFS, KS1 and KS2:

- EYFS will require smaller, lighter instruments that require less fine motor skill control.

- KS1 will require a range of untuned and tuned percussion instruments, the latter with note names or colour coding displayed for ease of use.

- As children progress through KS2 you will want to additionally provide instruments (or technology) on which they can play 'real' music of the type they hear outside school, such as guitars, keyboards and drums for performing pop music.

You also need to bear in mind the potential for instruments to get damaged, so it would be prudent to buy a few extra just in case... Similarly if the instruments require beaters, buy spares of these too. Triple the number required if you can, as these get bent, broken and lost with alarming alacrity!

Finally, you also need to consider the contents of your curriculum, in particular the different musical cultures you intend to explore. In order to give children an authentic experience of these musical cultures you will need authentic instruments, so you will want to make sure that your instrument collection encompasses a range of different musical cultures.

Top tip

Remember that the tools are only as good as the workman that wields them. If you are introducing new instruments into your school you will need to ensure that your colleagues know how to use them, otherwise they either won't get used, or children will learn to play them incorrectly. Fortunately this could make a really fun staff meeting activity as light relief in between all the updates and presentations, so you shouldn't have too much trouble getting your colleagues to participate!

Storing and transporting instruments

Some schools have a dedicated music room that classes come into for music, or have hall time allocated, but in many schools music teaching will happen in the classroom. Whichever set-up you have, you will have two main issues to address:

1. Where will you store all the instruments?
2. How will you get instruments from where they are stored to the music lessons?

Storing instruments

If money were no object, and storage space plentiful, then having a full set of tuned and untuned instruments for each class would be ideal. The closer these instruments are at hand, the more likely they are to be used! They will need to be stored in robust containers, ideally with individual compartments for each instrument so that you can see all the different types of instruments at a glance, and so that they are less likely to roll around on top of each other and get damaged.

You will also want to consider where the instruments children bring into school for their instrumental lessons are stored so that they are not accidentally trampled or bashed, and so that they are easy to locate in the inevitable eventuality that they get left at school overnight!

Transporting instruments

Most schools will not be lucky enough to have anywhere near the budget to achieve this though, so you will want a portable solution for your instruments to make it easier for teachers to access them – enter, creaking and rattling 'the music trolley!' A purpose-built music trolley is ideal for transporting instruments as long as you have somewhere safe to store it when it is not in use, and as long as your school does not have any stairs! If you need to transport instruments to different floors, then you will want to invest in boxes with handles that can be safely carried by children who you choose as 'instrument' monitors, as this will be much quicker than the teacher going up and down several times themselves to bring everything they need into the classroom.

Instrument maintenance

It is inevitable that over the course of time, instruments will get damaged. Fortunately, classroom percussion can often be fixed with everyday items like superglue, but orchestral instruments and similar may need a professional touch. The instrumental teacher may be able to carry out any minor repairs, and if not will be able to advise how best to proceed with finding a repair service. It would be worth auditing your instruments at the end of each term to identify any that need a little TLC before a minor problem becomes a major repair.

Music technology

Technology is ever evolving and the hardware and software available in schools varies greatly. A book such as this is therefore not the best place to attempt to support you with an overview of what might be available and how to use it, but it warrants a mention as technology can break down barriers to music-making for all children, and especially for those with additional needs. The best place to find up-to-date support is online, including the websites of the two subject associations for music education, the ISM and Music Mark.

Other useful resources

Ultimately, the resources that you may need will be dictated by the content of your curriculum and extra-curricular programmes, but below are some other suggestions of useful items that you might need. Remember that you will need to take some time to instruct your colleagues in how to use these resources in order to get the best out of them.

Copyright and licensing

As with physical property, it is important to be aware of others' intellectual property and understand when you need to obtain permission or a licence to include it in your music-making activities. The music licensing landscape and processes change from time to time, but the below list covers the main organisations and the types of usage they deal with. You can visit their websites to find out more.

- Printed Music Licencing Ltd (PMLL) – for copying or arranging sheet music from printed publications
- Performing Right Society Ltd (PRS) – for musical performances
- Phonographic Performance Ltd (PPL) – for playing recorded music
- The Mechanical Copyright Protection Society (MCPS) – for making CDs or DVDs
- Christian Copyright Licensing International (CCLI) – for projecting and copying Christian music

Conclusion

In this book, we have covered how to identify your vision for music in your school, and how to link this to your School Improvement Plan and get buy-in from your colleagues, children and parents. We have considered the content of your curriculum and extra-curricular programmes, and how these can be linked to create strong musical provision for your school. We have looked at the process of identifying your colleagues' learning needs, and supporting them on their journey to become better at teaching music. And we have looked at the resources needed to support musical activities within your school and how to ensure that these are used effectively.

Having read this book, you may now want to take some time to reflect on what needs to be done to develop and improve music in your school, and how you are going to go about addressing this. But please remember that you are just one person, you are probably not being paid additional money or given additional hours to fulfil your subject leader role, and you may have plenty of other responsibilities too. By reading this book you have started the journey towards revitalising music in your school; now take as much time as you need to establish your vision and turn it into a reality. It doesn't matter if it happens next week, next term, or next year, you are on your way, and that is all anyone can ask of you.

Bibliography and further reading

- Bamberger, J. (1991), *The Mind behind the Musical Ear: How children develop musical intelligence.* Cambridge, MA: Harvard University Press

- Benedict, C. (2006), 'Defining ourselves as other', in Frierson-Campbell, C. (ed) *Teaching Music in the Urban Classroom: A guide to survival, success and reform.* Blue Ridge Summit, PA: Rowman and Littlefield

- Charlton, K. (2020), *How to Teach Whole-class Instrumental Lessons: 50 inspiring ideas.* London: Collins

- Cultural Learning Alliance (2019), 'Arts GCSE and A Level Entries 2021' [Online] (**culturallearningalliance.org.uk/arts-gcse-and-a-level-entries-2021**)

- Department for Education (2016), *Standard for Teachers' Professional Development.* (**gov.uk/government/publications/standard-for-teachers-professional-development**)

- Durant, C. and Welch, G. (1995), *Making Sense of Music: Foundations for music education.* New York: Cassell

- Fautley, M. (2010), *Assessment in Music Education.* Oxford: OUP

- Fautley, M. (2019), 'Curriculum Planning & Classroom Music, *Primary Music Magazine 3.1*

- Fisher, R. (2008), 'Debating Assessment in Music Education'. *Research & Issues in Music Education 6 (1)*

- Hallam, S. (2015), *The Power of Music: a research synthesis of the impact of actively making music on the intellectual, social and personal development of children and young people.* London: iMerc

- Hargreaves, D. J., MacDonald, R. and Miell, D. (2011), 'Musical identities mediate musical development' in *Oxford Handbook of Music Education.* Oxford: OUP

- Harrison, D. (2017), *Abracadabra – Beginning Theory: Understanding the basics of music.* London: Collins

- Howard, K. and Hill, C. (2020), *Symbiosis: The curriculum and the classroom.* Melton: John Catt

- Kratus, J. (1991), 'Growing with Improvisation', *Music Educators' Journal 78*

- Mawby, S. L. (2018), 'Music in Schools for Children with Special Educational Needs: A Whole School Perspective'.

- Mills, J. (2005), *Music in the School.* Oxford: OUP

- Myatt, M. (2018), *The Curriculum: Gallimaufry to coherence.* Melton: John Catt

- Nicholls, S. and Hickman, S. (2021), *Collins Primary Music – Early Years Foundation Stage.* London: Collins

- Ofsted (2021), *Research review series: music* [Online] [Accessed 19/07/2021]

- Ofsted (2021), *School Inspection Handbook for September 2021* London: Ofsted

- Spruce, G (2007) 'Integration', *KS2 Music CPD Programme Study Guides* Milton Keynes: The Open University

- Sky Music Hub (2016), *WCET Best Practice Project.* (**skymusichub.com/the-hub/downloads**)

- Spruce, G. (2007), 'Integration' in *KS2 Music CPD Programme Study Guides.* Milton Keynes: The Open University.

- Stafford, E. J. V. (2021), 'Making a Model Music Curriculum: What's right for your school?' *Primary Music Magazine 5.2*

- Swanwick, K. (1988), *Music, Mind and Education.* London: Routledge

- Swanwick. K, (2012), *Teaching Music Musically.* Abingdon: Routledge

- Swanwick, K. and Tillman, J. (1986), 'The sequence of musical development: A study of children's composition', *British Journal of Music Education, 3 (3)*

- Welch, G. F. (2006), 'Singing and vocal development' in McPherson, G. *The Child as Musician: A handbook of musical development.* New York: OUP